Come away from the water, Shirley

Other books by John Burningham

John Burningham
Come away from the water, Shirley

RED FOX

A Red Fox Book

Published by Random House Children's Books
61-63 Uxbridge Road, London W5 5SA

A division of The Random House Group Ltd
Addresses for companies within The Random House Group Limited
can be found at : www.randomhouse.co.uk/offices.htm

Copyright © John Burningham 1977

7 9 10 8 6

First published in Great Britain by Jonathan Cape 1977

This Red Fox edition 2000

Printed in Singapore

THE RANDOM HOUSE GROUP Limited Reg. No. 954009

ISBN 978 0 099 89940 2

www.**rbooks**.co.uk

Of course it's far too cold for swimming, Shirley

We are going to put our chairs up here

Why don't you go and play with those children?

Mind you don't get any of that filthy tar on your nice new shoes

Don't stroke that dog, Shirley,
you don't know where he's been

That's the third and last time I'm asking you whether you want a drink, Shirley

Careful where you're throwing those stones.
You might hit someone.

You won't bring any of that smelly
seaweed home, will you, Shirley

Your father might have a game with you
when he's had a little rest

We ought to be getting back soon

Good heavens! Just look at the time.
We are going to be late if we don't hurry.